I0699784

Working Blue Press

Snowed In. Copyright © 2025 by Working Blue Press. All rights reserved. Printed in the United States of America. No part of this book may be used or reproduced in any manner without written permission except in the case of brief quotations embodied in critical articles and reviews. For permissions, information, and/or educational, business, or sales promotional use, please e-mail the marketing department at workingbluepress@gmail.com.

First Edition

ISBN 978-1-967038-16-9 (Kindle)
ISBN 978-1-967038-17-6 (Print)

For all the men and women who love
great sex, great relationships, and a
damn good time.

Content

Suggestions for Further Reading

Men Who Renovate Erotic Series
Books 1, 2, 3 and 4.

Follow Lacey Love on Amazon to keep abreast of new releases!

Snowed In

Men Who Renovate Erotic Series

Book 3

1

Snowed In

Jack wasn't quite sure what to say as the three other men stared at him. He dragged a rough hand through his hair, a piece falling across his eyes.

He was used to being the center of attention when it came to stories about sex and beautiful women. His whole college experience had been nothing but gorgeous women and enjoying everything the fairer sex had to offer.

But this time was different. For the first time in his life, he clamped up.

"So, wait a fuckin' minute here," Ben said. "You're telling me you're not going to get into any details about what happened in that log cabin with those two women?"

"You got it," Jack said.

"No, I call bullshit," Wolfe said.

"You're the guy women love to bang, Adonis, with those green eyes and black hair," Danny cracked. They all laughed. "Then we get to hear the stories. And now you're clamming up?"

Jack squirmed under their stares. They were right. He'd been *that* asshole in college. The one who bragged loudly and often about his sexual conquests. He loved sex, women loved to have sex with him, and so he enjoyed it.

Although, he was willing to admit now that he was older, that tt never felt particularly good to be *that* guy. Albeit it also didn't feel terrible. Either way, he was twenty-six years old now, his mother was gone, and he desperately wanted to shake that reputation.

But he didn't want an audience for it. Not yet. What he had to say was something he was happy about, not something he wanted to gossip about. It was something he'd only trust Wolfe with. At least for now.

"Alright, well, if we're not going to get anything good, I'm headed out," Ben said. He stood up and shoved his chair under the desk. "I need to get started on the small kitchen reno over on Bleak. They want it done before Christmas. Some paint and refinishing the cabinets, replacing the handles and faucets. So, I've got, what? Little more than a week?"

"Yeah, like ten days or so. I have a couple days before my consult if you need any help," Danny offered.

"Yeah, that'd be great, thanks," Ben said.

"Sure," Danny agreed. He stood up and tossed his coffee and trash from Dunkin' Donuts in the wastebasket. "Later, guys."

"Later," Wolfe said as Ben and Danny walked out.

"Yep, later," Jack said.

After the two left and the door shut, Jack glanced at Wolfe, who eyed him.

"So," Wolfe prodded. "What happened, man? Not like you to say nothin'."

Jack shrugged and then smiled.

"That doesn't look like nothing." Wolfe grinned. "It looks like how I looked after Gina and I hooked up."

"Maybe it is like that," Jack said. He shrugged.

"No shit, really?" Wolfe said. He leaned forward and raised an eyebrow. "You? A relationship? Holy shit. Talk."

Jack nodded. "Okay, here's what happened."

2

I Smell a Blizzard

Jack arrived at the log cabin in the North Carolina mountains shortly before noon on Friday as the sky began clouding up. He could swear he was still full from Thanksgiving dinner the day before at Wolfe and Gina's.

"That woman can cook," he whispered.

He shut off the engine and climbed out of his truck, grabbing his toolbox from the bed. He hadn't had time to listen to the weather report, but he heard a few locals talking something about snow in the mountains while he was grabbing his coffee and a little bundle of flowers at one of the gas stations a few miles up.

Didn't matter. He'd be in and out today. He just needed to drop off the final materials so he could get started on Monday after the holiday. Client wanted it to be done before Christmas and the family's annual holiday gathering.

"I thought you weren't starting until Monday?"

Jack turned quickly at the voice and gasped at the beauty before him, dropping his toolbox on his right foot in the process.

"Shit!" He winced as he turned and walked it off.

"Oh, shoot, I'm sorry," the gorgeous, brown-eyed blonde said as she rushed up to him. "Let me look."

She grabbed his arm and turned him around quickly as their eyes met and locked. He swore he heard her catch her breath, but he wasn't quite sure. He couldn't focus on much while her eyes were on him like that.

"Uh," she spit out. He smiled when she shook her head and refocused, then looked at him and grinned. "I'm a nurse."

"Oh," he said. "Okay."

Another moment of attraction zapped between them as she kneeled and gently undid his work boot, sliding it off.

"Steel toe," she quipped. "Good."

"Yeah, never leave home without 'em."

His ears tingled at her light laugh. It was a sweet, effervescent baritone that made a puff of white in the cold air, which now had a few snowflakes floating through it.

He took the second while she was pulling off his sock to notice her dark roots and blonde streaks—dark and light, which he liked. Her light blue sweater was pulled tight across her chest, showing off a gorgeous pair of breasts underneath. She was wearing low-cut, dark blue skinny jeans and knee-high Uggs.

He pulled in a breath as her delicate hands touched the top of his foot and then he winced.

She glanced up at him and he noticed she had three piercings in each ear, a mix of delicate gold balls, diamonds, and pearls.

"I think the corner hit the top of your foot here."

She pointed to a place high up his foot near his ankle, well past where the steel protection ended. It was already turning black and blue.

"I see that," he said.

"You need ice and compression," she said. "Help slow the bruising. And you probably should get an X-ray. There's an urgent care down the mountain. I can take you."

"Oh, no, I'll be fine," he said. "I've had much worse football injuries. I'll live."

He always liked to throw out he played football. It seemed to impress women.

"Ah," she said as she stood up and smiled.

But apparently not this woman.

"Okay, well," she said. "Can I at least wrap and ice it for you? I'd feel better."

"Sure," he said. He winced as he slipped his foot back in his boot and limped behind her as she turned to walk into the cabin. He had a bird's eye view of how perfect her ass looked in those jeans, and the way her waist came in and then jutted out at those lush hips.

She was stunning. And more importantly, she was kind. And even better, she was completely unimpressed by him and his usual antics.

"So, I didn't catch your name." They walked into the log cabin and he sat down on one of the kitchen chairs. It looked the same as when he'd been here a couple weeks ago with Colby Johnson, the man who owned this cabin and had hired him. Colby was old enough to be his dad. Was he hers?

"That's because I didn't tell you," she quipped. She got a plastic bag from the kitchen cabinet and held it under the ice dispenser of the fridge as it noisily dumped the cold cubes into their new home. "I know yours, though, Jack."

She sealed the plastic and dropped it on the counter as she walked out of the kitchen, down the hallway, and into the bathroom. He could hear her rustling around.

"Did Mr. Johnson tell you?" he asked. He heard her laugh as she came back with a compression wrap. She was grinning.

"Why's that funny?" he asked.

"It's always funny when people call my dad Mr. Johnson," she said. She kneeled and gently took his foot onto her leg as she wrapped it. She was good, too. Better than the football trainers in high school or college.

"Ah, so, this is a family cabin then?"

She nodded. "We've had it for years. We come and ski every Christmas. Friends and family use it, too. Like this weekend."

She grinned at him as she finished.

"I get it, you're here for the holiday weekend, then. I wasn't expecting anyone. I apologize for interrupting."

"You're not interrupting."

He caught her stare again and this time noticed bits of amber flecks in her brown eyes that gave a slight gold glow to her eyes. The sexual attraction between them was palpable, even though she seemed to be keeping her distance. He went to ask her name again, but a car pulled up. When Jack tried to glance out the window, he could see the snowflakes were coming down bigger and heavier.

"Wow, that, uh." He paused and looked a little harder. "That looks like a lot of snow."

"Yeah," she agreed. "I smell a blizzard."

"Smell what?" he asked.

"I can smell blizzards," she said. She shrugged. "I was surprised to see you, to be honest. Didn't you listen to the weather report?"

"Does my surprised face look like someone who listened to the weather report?"

He cracked a smile.

"Smart ass," she said. She loosened a little bit when he gave her a little bite. He liked that about her. She was the kind of woman who liked a little challenge. And definitely no bullshit. "Snowstorm moving in. About seven to twelve inches by five. More after that."

"A foot by five, huh?" He glanced back out the window. "I should get my stuff unloaded and then head out."

A car door slammed and a few seconds later the front door swung open. In its frame was a gorgeous raven-haired beauty with snow in her hair and across the black jacket on her small shoulders. She yanked off her sunglasses revealing deep blue eyes.

"What up, bitch?" she yelled. In response, his blonde-haired beauty gave a girl scream. They rushed each other and hugged.

Chicks, man. He didn't get it. But he couldn't deny the pleasure of seeing women touching each other. Especially hot women like these two.

"What is this snow oh my gawd?" the brunette beauty said. "Perfect for our weekend."

"Totally," the blonde said.

Finally, the new friend noticed him.

"Oh hello, and you are?"

"The help," the blonde quipped. She gave him a little wink.

"I'm Jack," he said. He gave the blonde an eye roll as he reached out his hand to the brunette. She was equally hot, her slender figure obvious in her leggings and snow boots. "I'm doing a renovation here."

"Today?" she asked confused.

"Monday. I was dropping off tools and final materials," he said. "I didn't actually know anyone would be here."

"Well, surprise, surprise," she
cooed. She let go of his hand and
slipped off her jacket revealing
large, ample breasts barely hidden
in her V-neck tight pink sweater.
"Ariel, whatever will we do with
our…" — she glanced at his
quickly swelling foot—"…injured
help?"

"Ariel?" he quickly looked to the
blonde and saw her dark eyes
sparkle.

"Well, now you know," she said.

He held her stare for a second
too long and couldn't help but
notice how his body reacted to her
in a way he hadn't quite felt before.
Yeah, he'd had a lot of sex. He'd
also had a lot of girlfriends. But
what his body was feeling toward
Ariel was some combination of the
two, plus something else.

What was that something else?

"How about we help you unload
your truck? It'll go faster. Then you

can get outta here before the roads
back down the mountain get too
bad." Ariel grabbed her coat, slid it
on and zipped it up before he could
move.

"Yeah, no, that's not
happening," he said. He slid his
sock and boot on quickly as he
stood. It hurt like hell, but he was
not about to let women haul his
tools. "My mama would kill me if I
let you do that."

"Oh, come on," Ariel scoffed.

"Hang on, the 1950s are calling
my phone," the brunette said as she
peered at her phone. The two girls
looked at each other, then him, and
laughed. "We're capable women,
caveman Jack."

"I didn't say you weren't," he
said quickly. "I promise you, I'm
not that guy. I know women can do
all that stuff. I would never say you
couldn't. But, for one thing, it's a
liability for my business if you do,

so legally, you can't. And, again, my mom taught me better."

"Well, your mom's not here, so." Ariel laughed and then she stopped almost immediately. His face must have betrayed him. A mistake he usually didn't make, but it was the holidays, and he missed his mom, so her memory was top-of-mind. A fresh wound even though it'd been two years already.

"Did I say something wrong?" she asked quickly.

He shook it off as he glanced out the window. The snow was really coming down now. He glanced back at her. "I really do need to unload. I'll move as fast as I can."

They both nodded as he limped toward the door.

"Cara."

He turned around to the brunette. "I'm sorry?"

"My name. It's Cara. Ariel and Cara."

"Gotcha," he said. He grinned at them. "Nice to meet you both."

"You, too," Cara said.

"Jack—"

"It's cool, Ariel," he said. "This won't take me long, then I'll be out of your hair."

He smiled as if nothing was wrong and walked out into the snow that was already three inches deep.

All he had to do was unload his truck and then he could head home. He had a Hungry Man frozen dinner and Gina's leftover pumpkin pie waiting for him.

And if he had enough time, he'd stop at the cemetery.

He needed to put the flowers he'd bought on his mom's grave. To make it look nice for the holidays.

And maybe, just maybe, he'd tell her about this girl, Ariel, he met,

who was making him feel
something he'd never felt before.
   And, damn, did he like it.

3

Cold Nights, Hot Tubs

Jack would never outright admit it, but his foot was killing him. And walking on it was only making it swell more. It didn't help he'd slipped three times on the way in and out of the front door. After the first two times, the girls got embarrassed for him and left. He had no idea where they went, but he was glad he was alone so he could swear and carry on about his dumb luck.

"Fuckin' snow," he hissed. He slipped again, grabbing the side of his truck as he reached for the final paint cans, grabbed them, and yanked them out of the truck. This was the last of it. It was closing in on two o'clock. If it hadn't been snowing, if he hadn't hurt his foot, he'd have been gone by now. But as it was, the snow was already half a foot deep and getting deeper. He needed to leave soon, or he wouldn't be able to leave at all.

Not that a Friday night with Ariel and Cara would be a bad thing. But it wouldn't be the way he'd want to do it with Ariel. He wanted to take her out to dinner. Like a real first date, not "hanging out." Not like his usual dates as a college-aged man.

Jack was a professional man now. He wanted to ask Ariel for her number, text her, take her out, open her car door, buy her dinner. That romantic stuff. Stuff he had half-assed when he was twenty with young women who went on to marry other men. Ariel was different. He wanted to show her that.

"Hello?" he asked. He walked inside the cabin, set the paint down and shut the door. He took his boots off, feeling some relief on his right foot when he did, and walked in a little bit more. "Ariel? Cara?"

Where the hell could they have gone?

"Hey."

He knew it was Cara before he turned around. When he did, his eyes flew open. The yellow bikini she was sporting was so tiny he wasn't entirely sure she was wearing anything at all. She walked right up to him, so close that her nipples were brushing against his jacket.

"Uh." He barely got the utterance out of his mouth.

"We're going in the hot tub out back. Wanna join us?"

The clear answer was yes. Of course he wanted to go in the hot tub. Good God, look at this woman. She was clearly his type of woman when he was in college, and she knew that, as evidenced by her nipples now nearly pressing through his jacket to his chest. His cock was knocking on his zipper begging to be let loose from its cage, like a prize fighter ready for the ring.

But…Ariel. He took a step back.

"I didn't realize there was a hot tub," he said. Shit, that was close. His old self, the college guy, the twenty-something without a care in the world before his mother died was trying to resurface. He liked that guy. He was fun and carefree.

"Oh, yeah, it's nice and hot," she purred. She stepped right back to him, her nipples against his jacket once more. She was persistent. And he loved that.

"Oh yeah," he said quietly.

"Yeah." She trailed her fingers up his jacket and toyed with the scruff on his chin. "You are…very sexy, Jack."

"What's going on?"

When Jack glanced at Ariel, his whole body responded. She was wearing a black, string bikini that stretched perfectly across her hips. The top held her gorgeous, perky breasts in a way that made him want to pull the material aside and take her hard nipples in his mouth.

"Nothing," he said quickly.

"Well, not nothing," Cara cooed. "I'm trying to get him in the hot tub with us."

A look passed between the girls before Ariel's gaze landed on him. The heat from her stare damn near melted him right there.

"Yeah," she agreed. "Come in the hot tub with us."

There was no way in hell he was turning Ariel down. But…the snow.

"I'd love to but…" he glanced out the large windows at the front and could see the snow was halfway up his tires now. He looked back at them. "If I stay, I'll be here at least overnight. The storm."

He nodded to the windows and both girls looked, then peered back at him.

"I don't see any problem with that," Cara said. "Do you, Ariel?"

Ariel paused for a second as a glance passed between them. He wasn't sure what it was. Then it was gone and replaced with a sultry smile.

"I have no problem with that," Ariel said. She walked over to him and unzipped his jacket, sliding it off him. Her hands on him like that made his cock so hard he couldn't move. As her arms moved his coat off and then started unbuttoning his shirt, he could smell some sort of floral or vanilla. Her scent was amazing and all he could think of was how she might taste.

"How's your ankle?" she whispered. She slid his shirt off him, her lips coming dangerously close to his.

He smiled at her. "It'll be fine."

"Let me look." She brushed her cute nose against his as she unbuckled his jeans. She slid them down his legs, revealing his firm cock inside his boxer briefs, as he stepped out of his pants. He winced as he pulled his right foot out and set it down. Even with the compression bandage, it had swollen up pretty good.

"Oh my God," she exclaimed. She looked up at him. "Jack, you need to elevate this foot and get ice on it."

She was right. He did need to get off that foot, and he probably wouldn't be able to drive with it, either.

"I'll put him in the hot tub to relax while you get him ice," Cara said. She winked at him.

Ariel stood up and eyed her friend, then nodded. "Yeah, okay."

She gave him another look that he couldn't quite decipher but he agreed. Now that he was starting to relax, he could really feel his foot thumping.

When she turned to walk away, he said, "Ariel, wait."

She glanced at him.

"Are you sure it's okay…that I stay?"

She smiled at him. "Yeah, I'm sure."

"Okay." One more look and she was in the kitchen getting the ice as Cara took his hand and led him to the other side of the cabin he hadn't seen yet. She took his gimpy ass down a small hallway to the master bedroom.

"Big bed," Cara said softly. She peered at him over her shoulder with those stunning blue eyes as he limped behind her. "Enough for three."

He grinned at her. She was sexy as fuck in that bikini, and he definitely wanted to run his hands all over her body. He wanted Ariel, too. In truth, he already knew, he wanted Ariel the most.

They stepped through the glass doors from the master bedroom onto an attached patio where the hot tub was already bubbling hot with steam rising from it. The snow was falling and evaporating all around it.

Cara led him to the steps, then let go of his hand and carefully stepped into the tub. Before she was all the way in, she turned to face him and slowly removed her bikini top exposing her beautiful tits with a smile. She threw the top on the deck and reached out her hand.

"Come on, Jack," she purred.

He grinned. She was like a mythical siren of the sea, and he was all in. He took her hand and stepped gingerly into the tub, one foot at a time, his right foot screaming at him to get off it as the snow fell.

The hot, steamy water felt amazing in the cold, snowy environment as he sunk down into the tub and took a seat.

"Let's get that foot up." Cara's nipples grazed the water as her hand reached in for his leg. She helped him raise it onto one of the steps, so it was elevated, with the injured part out of the water.

"Better?" she asked huskily.

Her hot stare could melt steel as he gazed down her throat to her heavy breasts. His cock hardened as he watched her pink buds dip in

and out of the water with her
movements. He glanced back to her
eyes as they fixated on his. He felt
her soft hand trailing up his right
leg under the water. The closer her
fingers inched to his manhood, the
harder he got inside his briefs.

"Does this feel good?" she
asked.

"Mmmhmm," he murmured as
his eyes got heavy. Now her hand
was on his inner thigh and her
delicious breasts were only a
couple inches from his mouth.
They were calling to him. As her
fingers reached his balls and started
stroking them, her nipples were
right at his mouth and he pulled
one in, sucking on the delicious
pink nub as she moaned.

"Fuck," she murmured. She slid
her free hand into his hair and
directed his mouth as he sucked
and licked first one tit, then the
other. Her hand was firm around

his balls as she stroked them before moving to his thick cock.

"Thanks, yeah," Ariel said on the other side of the glass door just before she opened it.

He quickly pulled back from Cara as Ariel hung up her cell phone and dropped it on a side table by the door. She walked outside with ice, water, and something else in her hand, then slid the door shut. She stopped when she saw Cara with her top off and him with his foot elevated. She grinned.

"I see the party's started," she said, her voice smokey with desire. She captured his gaze and held it as she walked over and put the ice on his foot. She stepped into the hot bubbling water and when she got to the last step, she untied her bikini top with her free hand and tossed it to the side by Cara's.

"Oh god," he uttered as he took in her full, round breasts, the rose buds standing at attention. He wanted nothing more than to have them in his mouth. As if reading his mind, she moved gently through the water to him as Cara stepped to the left and sat next to him. Ariel stepped between his legs.

"Advil," she said. She unclenched her hand and revealed the pain meds. "Open."

He opened his mouth and she gently used her free hand to take the pills and place them on his tongue, holding his hot stare as she did. She cracked open the water bottle and handed it to him. He gently took the bottle and swallowed a large drink of water along with the pills. She smiled, took the water, recapped it, and set aside.

"Thank you," he whispered. She closed the distance and stood before him, her breasts right at his mouth as her hands dipped into the water.

"You're welcome," she said quietly. Her hands grazed his chest. And for a moment, it felt like only the two of them were there. It felt perfect.

"Ariel," he said so low, he didn't think she heard him. He knew Cara didn't, who slid right next to him and started kissing his neck as Ariel leaned forward and ran her hands down his chest. He took the opportunity to pull her nipples into his mouth as he ran his hands up her tight ass and back.

She gasped as she leaned down and kissed him deeply. He couldn't stop the moan it elicited from his chest as one of her hands found his cock and the other found his hair. She pulled his head back and sank her tongue into his mouth.

He slid one hand to her breasts and thumbed her nipple as his other hand found her slick opening and slid a finger inside, then another. She pulled away from the kiss with a groan as he thrust his fingers deeper. She held his gaze as he pleasured her, his thumb on her clit, rubbing and circling it.

He let out a moan as her hand stroked his cock.

"Ariel," he whispered. "Yes."

She smiled at him then and it again felt like it was just the two of them even though Cara was suckling his neck and chest with her hand stroking his balls.

He could feel his orgasm rising as Ariel leaned in close to his mouth. They were breathing the same air as he pounded her pussy with deep finger thrusts. "Come," he whispered.

"Yes," she whispered back to him. She captured his gaze and

nodded to him that she was
coming.

She gripped his hair with one
hand and stroked him harder with
the other.

"I'm coming," he panted.

"Come," she ordered.

As his salty release coated his
chest, he could feel her pussy grip
his fingers. Cara licked up his neck
as she let go of his balls and started
to clean up him and the water.

"Look at ya," Cara said silkily.
She grinned as she stood up and
sloshed out of the water. "I'll get
towels."

As Cara went inside, he locked
eyes with Ariel, pulled his fingers
out as she let go of his cock, and he
pulled her onto his lap. It felt
incredible to hold her there as the
water gurgled around them and the
snow fell magically around them.
She slid her arms around his neck

and leaned against his chest as she straddled him.

It was quiet and simple as her breathing slowed with his.

"There's somethin' about you, Jack," she whispered in his ear.

He smiled when she said it and his heart leapt into his throat. He pulled her closer and tighter to him as he closed his eyes and let the magic of the moment wash over them. He didn't know what this was, but he already knew he didn't ever want to let it go.

4

Locked In

Ariel had thought it was Cara when Jack pulled up to the cabin. But as soon as she saw the truck, she knew it was the man her dad had hired for the kitchen renovation. She hadn't expected him until Monday, but her dad had told her he may be in and out to drop off supplies and materials.

So, she'd thought nothing of it when she hollered at him. But when he turned around and she caught those green eyes and black hair, she had to catch her breath. And then he damn near broke his foot with that toolbox. Helping him after that had given her a million feels.

When he had looked in her eyes, she had been immediately drawn in. It was like a magnet pulling on her and she couldn't pull away. When the snow started to fall, she was grateful. She wanted him stuck there with her. She wanted to know everything there was to know about Jack.

And then Cara arrived, and she had seen that Cara wanted him, too. But there was no way in hell she was going to let her best friend have Jack. So, when he'd unloaded the truck by himself, she had dragged Cara back to the master bedroom.

"He's mine," Ariel had said.

"Oh, come on, you just met him," Cara had protested. "You couldn't possibly know you want him all to yourself yet."

"I do know, Cara, I'm telling you, I want you to back off, seriously, please," she had practically begged. Not that there was a choice. Ariel had felt confident that even though Jack was obviously attracted to Cara, he wanted her. The pull between them was too strong.

"Ariel, look—"

"Cara," she had interrupted.

Cara had raised her hands then and backed off with a wide grin. "Wow, you really like him."

"I mean, too early to like him, like him," Ariel had said. "But there's definitely *something*."

"Fine," Cara had retorted. "But I wanna play with him a little bit, too."

"Cara!"

"Delta Gamma Theta party, freshmen year, I let you make-out with my boyfriend because you didn't believe me when I said his lips were soft," Cara had asserted. She had put her hands on her hips.

Ariel had huffed a sigh. "Fine. But no kissing him and no touching his dick and no fucking him."

"Deal." Cara had smiled.

"You get him for five minutes alone in the hot tub and after we're done in the hot tub, that's it," Ariel had said. "We'll convince him to stay long enough until the roads are closed, then he's mine."

"Done."

And then they had both slid on their bikinis, ready to tempt him into staying, which hadn't been hard. She knew as soon as he saw her in her bikini that he had wanted her. So, she did as she promised and gave Cara her five minutes and then Jack had been hers.

The sexual part had been amazing, and his cock was perfect, thick and long. But it was what happened after, when Cara left, and he had pulled her to him that left her breathless.

They had stayed like that for a
few minutes until Cara came back
and announced the roads down the
mountain were closed until at least
tomorrow, maybe Sunday. He had
smiled at her, and she knew he was
okay with being there with her as
well.

Once they had dried off and put
clothes on, she threw all their wet
clothes, including his boxer briefs,
into the washer and dryer. She
could hear the dryer now as she and
Jack stood in the kitchen together
making dinner. Cara was on her
laptop watching a movie in her
room.

"So," she said. She eyed him in
his work jeans and dark blue T-
shirt. "Spaghetti is your
masterpiece?"

He grinned as he limped from
the cupboard to the island, holding
spices in his hand before sitting

them down next to the fresh tomatoes.

"Just watch and be amazed," he cracked. His smile was so sexy she got immediately wet.

"Okay," she said. She shrugged. "Can I pour you a glass of wine?"

"That'd be great," he said. "And do you have garlic bread by chance?"

"Hang on," she said. She opened the freezer. "We do, I can't believe it."

She pulled out the loaf of frozen garlic bread. "Want me to heat up the oven?"

"Would you?"

"Of course," she said. He glanced over his shoulder and a dark hair fell across his green eyes as he smiled.

"Thank you," he said softly.

"You're welcome." She felt a glow of heat rush up her neck to her face. This man…oh this man.

She was in trouble. She turned on the oven, pulled out a sheet tray, and pulled the loaf of garlic bread out of its packaging. She split it open and put it on the metal pan.

"Ready for the oven," she said.

"Awesome."

She went to the pantry and selected a red wine, grabbed a couple of Solo cups, and walked back to the island. She put the red cups down and cracked open the wine as he started laughing.

"Holy shit, Solo cups," he teased. "I don't think I've seen one of those since college."

She laughed, too, glad that he was so light-hearted about it.

"I know, right?" she said. She poured the rich, dark merlot into the cups, then handed a cup to him and picked hers up. "Cheers."

"Cheers." As they each took a sip, their eyes met over the rims of their cups and twinkled with humor.

"Ah," he said as he put his cup down. "Wine out of a plastic cup. Drink of champions."

"Shut it." She laughed as she put her cup down and slid onto the island next to where he was cooking. They snuck glances at each other as he skillfully cut the tomatoes into a saucepan that already had water and a few other things.

"Wow, you actually do know how to cook," she commented. "Where'd that come from?"

"My mama," he said quietly.

"She a chef?"

"She was, yes."

"Was?"

He paused for a second as he put the last of the tomatoes in the pan and added the spices. He put the pan on the island burner and turned on the heat, stirring the ingredients together. He finally looked right at her.

"My mom died of breast cancer two years ago," he said.

"Oh my God, Jack," she said quickly. Her eyes immediately misted over. As a nurse, she had seen patients battle breast cancer, die from breast cancer, none of it was pretty. All of it was hard. "I'm so sorry. And I said that stupid thing about your mother earlier, oh my God."

She buried her face in her hands as the tears hit her eyes. She immediately felt his arms around her.

"It's okay, Ariel, you didn't know."

"I feel like an asshole."

His rich laugh helped pull her tears back. "You're not an asshole."

He pulled her hands down from her face and wiped away the

forming tears, holding her gaze for a bit too long before bending down and giving her a light kiss.

Electricity shot her through body as the softness of his lips brushed against hers. When he pulled back, he looked into her eyes as he tucked a loose hair behind her ear.

"She was diagnosed my junior year of college," he said. He stepped away and stirred the sauce. "She did all the treatments. Chemo, radiation. She did those cold cap things."

"Ouch," she whispered.

"Yeah," he said. He exhaled a deep breath. "She went into remission for a year. Then it came back. When it did, it had metastasized into her brain. Kidneys. Everywhere."

She wanted to die a little at the pain in his eyes when he looked at her.

"You've seen it, yeah? Someone die from breast cancer?"

She nodded as tears bit the back of her eyes.

"She got to see me graduate college," he said. He swiped at his eyes. "That's all she wanted. Just for me to get a degree. But…she won't see me get married. Or have children of my own."

He stirred the sauce again.

"Be a grandma," he said quietly, finishing some thought he was having.

"Jack," she breathed. She could barely keep it together. "What was her name?"

"Kate. Kate Glass."

"Pretty."

He glanced at her, and a smile passed between them.

"Your dad seems very cool," he said.

"He is," she said. "Him and my mom. Married for thirty years."

"You have brothers? Sisters?"

"Two sisters and a brother," she said.

"Big family. You're lucky."

"No siblings?"

"Just me and my mom," he said. "That's it."

He stirred the sauce again and she could now smell it as it wafted through the kitchen.

"That smells amazing."

He turned the heat down on the burner. "It needs to simmer."

He walked over to her, and his eyes were dark with attraction as he slid his hands up her bare thighs and just under her shorts. It zapped her right in her pleasure zone to feel his fingers start lightly rubbing her skin.

"You're easy to talk to," he said lightly.

She slid her hands up his arms, to his neck and cupped his face. "So are you," she whispered.

She leaned in and kissed him, soft at first, then as her hormones heated up, a little rougher, the passion rising.

"I'm glad I didn't listen to the weather report, or I might not have come," he said. He ran one hand into her hair and gently pulled as he kissed her deeply. A moan escaped her mouth as the feeling of his strength and masculinity radiated through her body.

"I'm glad you didn't, either," she said between kisses. "Jack."

She moaned as his other hand made its way from her thigh up her long-sleeved, fitted white shirt then under her bra. The feeling of his rough hands squeezing and stroking the delicate skin of her breast made her squirm with pleasure. She arched her body toward him, using her knees to grip his hips and pull him toward her.

"Ariel," he breathed as he shoved her shirt and bra up and dipped his head down to take her nipple into his mouth.

"Yes," she panted as he sucked and licked her pink buds at an achingly slow pace. "More."

At that, he took a slight step back forcing her to unwrap her legs from his waist. Then his hands made their way down to the waistband of her athletic shorts and pulled them down and off her body.

"Yes," she moaned. She spread her legs wide and he stepped between them. She made an animalistic noise as he stroked the insides of her thighs and took in her beautifully shaved and groomed pussy.

"Fuck," he moaned. "I bet you taste amazing."

At that, he dove between her legs, pushing them further back so he could get deeper inside her with his tongue. He dipped and licked and sucked until she was squirming underneath his magical touch.

It wasn't enough for him, though. He took one hand and slid it up her abdomen, fondling her breast, and used the other hand to slide his fingers deep inside her.

She almost came undone as he fingered her while he ate her out.

She had never felt so much pleasure in all her life. Jack wasn't going down on her just to get her wet and fuck her, he was taking his time, making sure she felt pleasured. It was intense and she could feel her powerful orgasm gathering in her pelvis and ready to tumble over.

"Jack!" She started to squirm as she grabbed the edges of the island. "Jack, I'm gonna come!"

As soon as she said that he intensified his efforts, skillfully fondling her breasts, stroking her

G-spot, and sucking her clit, all at the same time. It was too much. She couldn't stop the roaring waves of pleasure as they overtook her.

"Jack!" Screaming his name felt like the most natural thing in the world as his hands, fingers, and mouth explored every inch of her eager body. She wanted more—many more—moments just like this.

As she came down from her high, she could feel Jack's hands lightly stroking her abs and her thighs as he kissed her pussy gently, then her inner thighs. She reached between her legs and touched his face as he gazed up at her.

"That was amazing," she whispered.

He grinned at her as he stood straight and helped her sit up. He grabbed her shorts and helped slide them back on her, then he pulled her into another hug and laid his head on her shoulder as he exhaled.

"You're amazing, Ariel," he said quietly into her ear.

She wrapped her legs around him and pulled him close.

She didn't know what they had started while snowed in at her family's log cabin, but whatever it was, she felt like it was something she never wanted to let go of.

And she hoped he felt the same way, too.

5

Magical

Waking up with Ariel in his arms, her sleek, naked body held tightly to his own, was the best feeling he'd ever had in his life. Peering out the sliding glass doors to the master bedroom's patio where three feet of glistening snow had piled up made it even more magical.

He had never in his life felt this way about a woman, and certainly not this quickly, but everything was different with Ariel. He kissed her neck gently as he cuddled her from behind. She gave a little moan and pushed back into his body, and he pulled her even closer.

She had made that little moan last night, too. Several times. After dinner, the three of them had played cards and drank wine while they laughed and talked. It had become very clear, very quickly that Cara knew he was off-limits, and so he was free to give all his attention to Ariel, which is where he wanted to direct it.

Ariel wasn't like anyone he had ever met. She was intelligent, kind, and had a wicked sense of humor that matched his own. It seemed there was no end to the depth of her character. He could tell she gave a shit about people and her job as a nurse. He knew in his gut that his mother would have loved Ariel.

His gut was also telling him that Ariel was going to be special to him, and so he treated her accordingly.

After Cara went to bed, the two of them had shared a passionate kiss and when she had pulled back from it, she had whispered, "Take me to bed or lose me forever."

They had both laughed at the classic line from the original Top Gun, his favorite movie, and hers, too.

So that's exactly what he had done.

"Jack, yes," she had moaned as he had laid her down on the bed in the master suite. He had slowly kissed down her throat to her breasts and abs. He slid his hands down her body and slowly slid her tank top off. "Yes, baby."

He unhooked the front latch of her lacy little bra and as her breasts tumbled out, he grabbed them with his hands and kneaded them as his thumbs massaged her nipples.

"Jack," she had whispered as she reached her hands down into his hair and pulled on it with pleasure.

He kissed down further and slid his hands down to her shorts again and pulled them off as he kissed her sweet, tight pussy, then down her thighs, and finally pulled off her shorts as he stood up.

"Fuck," he had whispered as he'd gazed down at her beautiful body. She had been completely relaxed, looking at him with those dark eyes, giving him all her trust. It had made his heart contract in a way he had never experienced before. He wanted her trust, wanted to keep it, wanted to prove he was capable of it. "You're beautiful."

She had smiled at him then and sat up, sliding to the end of the bed and grabbing his T-shirt. She had lifted it and kissed his stomach as she stood and took it off, kissing him up his chest to his neck. When she had pulled the T-shirt over his head, he had kissed her deeply, and that perfect little moan escaped her throat when he did.

"You're amazing," she had whispered to him, as she kissed down his chest again. He had entangled his hand in her hair as she landed at his belt, unbuckling it, and opening his jeans, pulling his jeans down and letting his hard, thick cock free.

"Ariel," he had said hoarsely as her hands slid up his thighs and grabbed his ass as she licked and teased the tip of his cock, swallowing his salty pre-come.

"You taste so good," she had whispered.

"Fuck," he had whispered. He could barely hang on seeing her like that as she slid her hands around his hips, one grabbing the base of his cock, the other stroking his balls. When she had pulled the whole tip of his manhood into her mouth, he groaned with pleasure.

"Ariel," he panted as she had pulled his cock deeper into her throat, her eyes sparkling with pleasure as she watched him. Her hand gripped his cock and stroked it as her mouth worked the shaft making him harder than he'd ever been in his life.

"Ariel, stop," he ordered. "Or else I'll come, please."

She had stopped then with a wicked little smile and slid back onto the bed, lying down, and spreading her legs for him as she eagerly writhed her hips.

"I want you, Jack," she had whispered huskily.

"I want you, too, baby," he had said. And he did. He wanted her to be his baby, to be his, to know her better, to find out who this woman—this intoxicating woman who held his heart in her hands already—was and what they might be together.

He had slid onto the bed between her legs then and positioned himself at her entrance. He had leaned down and looked into her eyes, then kissed her gently as he pushed the tip of his cock inside her slick opening.

"Jack," she had panted. She had looked deep in his and his heart had melted. Her gaze was trusting, beautiful, and ready for him. It was exactly the same stare he was giving back to her.

"Ariel," he had whispered as he had slowly and gently slid all the way inside her.

"Oh God!" She had slid her hands in his hair and gripped as he started thrusting inside of her. "Yes, baby, yes!"

"Ariel," he had panted. He had known he wasn't going to last long, and neither was she. The build-up between them was so intense, they could barely hang on as he thrust harder and harder.

He had kissed her and nuzzled into her neck as she moaned with pleasure.

"Harder, baby, please!"

"Yes, baby," he had said. And he had rocked against her pussy, his balls slamming into her ass giving her pleasure in every place he could. He slid his hand down and started thumbing her nipple as he felt his orgasm tighten in his pelvis.

"Fuck me, Jack," she had ordered. "Harder, baby."

He had sat up then and grabbed her hips, raising them so he could get a new angle and rocked hard against her.

"Oh fuck, right there!" She had squirmed then, grabbing the pillows behind her head as he thrust over and over again.

"Right there, baby?" he had asked.

"God yes, I'm coming!"

And they had locked eyes as both of their orgasms rose to their ultimate heights then crashed against their bodies as they each moaned, coming with the other.

"Ariel, fuck," he had said, and he had let go and laid against her as the final waves of pleasure washed over them both.

They each had laughed gently as their breathing had started to return to normal.

He had laid there on her chest for a minute as she slid her hands into his hair and kissed the side of his face gently.

"Jack," she whispered. "That was perfect."

"It really was," he had whispered back.

He had lifted his head and looked in her eyes. "Ariel, this means something to me."

She had smiled at him then and whispered back, "Me, too."

He had kissed her gently and when he pulled back she had said, "I haven't started to fall this quickly for someone…like, ever."

He had laughed then, relieved she was in the same place. "Me, either," he had said. "But it's happening."

"It is," she had said. They had kissed some more and then he had pulled her into his arms, and they had fallen asleep.

And now it was morning on a magical snowy day in a log cabin in the mountains, and he was the happiest he had ever been in his life.

He kissed her neck again and this time, her eyelids fluttered open. She glanced at him with a smile and his heart skipped for a second. He hoped to God she still felt the same way in the cold light of day as she did last night.

"Jack," she whispered. "Morning."

"Morning," he said quietly. He gave her a gentle kiss.

They both laughed a little.

"I'm so glad you got stuck here," she said quietly.

Thank God she still felt the same way. His heart surged with joy.

"Me, too," he said. He grinned at her. "So, a little late but, do you think, once we get outta here, I can take you on a date?"

She laughed, then gazed at him. "Wasn't last night basically a first date? And also, maybe a second and third?"

They both laughed together as he kissed her shoulder, then her lips.

"I guess, maybe, yes," he said. "So, the better question might be, I'd like to keep seeing you. If you'd like to keep seeing me?"

She nodded as she gently kissed him. "I'd like that."

"Good," he said as he kissed her again. "I should probably get your phone number then."

She laughed again and he knew he'd never get tired of that sound as long as he lived.

"You can have my number and anything else you want," she purred.

"Is that right?"

"That's right," she said. She gave him a sexy stare.

"Oh, well then, let me get right to what I want right now." He playfully jumped on top of her and kissed her neck as she laughed right along with him.

He had an inkling that what he had started with Ariel, wherever it led, it was exactly where he needed to be.

She was a game-changer. And he couldn't wait to see where it led.

6

Business or Pleasure?

Jack smiled at Wolfe as his friend eyed him with a happy grin.

"Jack," he started. He shook his head, then glanced at his buddy with happiness. "Man, I could not be happier for you, seriously."

Jack grinned with relief from ear to ear. This kind of relationship with Ariel was new for him, and Wolfe knew that. Jack had had "girlfriends," but he'd never had a *girlfriend*. One that he could envision the "L" word with.

But he could envision that and more with Ariel. And that was new for him, so he wasn't quite sure how to handle it.

"Thanks, man," Jack said.

"Listen, I know this isn't what you've typically had in the past," Wolfe said. "But, trust me, you'll know what to do as you go. If it's for real, it'll just happen. And you won't have to do anything except let it happen."

"Okay," Jack nodded. Wolfe had been his friend since college. Most guys had thought Jack was a big player and never took him totally seriously. Wolfe hadn't. Wolfe had a way of seeing people, seeing through them. He appreciated that about his friend. "Thanks."

"Sure." A quiet moment passed before Wolfe spoke again. "You think Mama Glass would like her?"

Jack laughed. Only the four of them called his mom, "Mama Glass." She had always loved it when the four of them had shown up at the house. Even sick, she would get up and make them a meal, and laugh when they had called her Mama Glass.

"She would," Jack said quietly.

"Good," Wolfe said. "Seems to me like that's all you really need to know."

Jack couldn't help the tears that clouded his vision for a second as Wolfe reached out and slapped his shoulder.

"Listen, how about you and Ariel come have dinner with me and Gina?"

Jack wiped his eyes and grinned at his friend. "Yeah, that'd be great."

"Cool," Wolfe said. "I mean, Gina can't cook like you, maestro."

"Hey, her Thanksgiving meal was pretty damn good."

"I know, right?" Wolfe wiggled his eyebrows as they both laughed. "She can whip up something great, though. We can play some cards.

Meet this dream girl of yours, huh?"

Jack grinned. He knew Wolfe would understand his desire to move slowly with something so new to him and to Ariel. He appreciated it. "Thanks, man, yes, that'd be great."

Wolfe nodded. "This one was truly business *and* pleasure."

"Totally."

"And the reno turned out beautifully," Wolfe said.

"It did," Jack said. "Her dad was really happy with it."

"Is her dad happy about the other part?" Wolfe grinned.

"Yeah, maybe a little less happy about that," Jack said. "But he's cool. He did tell Ariel to invite me to their Christmas shenanigans, so I guess that's a good sign."

"Dude, really?" Wolfe asked. A look of concern crossed his face, then a smile. "So, you have somewhere to be for the holiday, then?"

Jack nodded as he glanced at the ground, then his friend.

"Good," Wolfe said.

"Ariel said she'd come with me. To my mom's grave."

"She sounds like a great girl."

Jack nodded. His heart felt fuller than it had since before his mom died. "Thanks for coming up with this idea, man. You know, the side hustle. The renovations. It's, uh, turning out to really be something great."

"It is, isn't it?" Wolfe asked with a nod. "Who would have guessed?"

"Not me, dude, I thought it was gonna fail right from the start."

"Oh, fuck you, man." Wolfe laughed as he stood and gave Jack a punch on the arm.

Jack laughed as he stood with his friend. "Wanna go get breakfast?"

"Yeah, let's do it."

Jack smiled as he followed Wolfe out of the office.

For the first time in a long time, he felt like he could breathe again. And he knew this friendship, this business, and now Ariel, were to thank for all of it.

Jack's sexy story with Ariel isn't over! Keep reading the *Men Who Renovate Erotic Series* to see what happens to him and his sexy friends! Wanna learn more about the other men—Danny, Wolfe, and Ben? Keep reading the *Men Who Renovate Erotic Series* as they build their business, enjoy sex, and talk about it all!

Scan me

<u>**Review this book!**</u>

Do you love *Snowed In* as part of
the *Men Who Renovate Erotic
Series*? Then tell everyone about it!
Leave a review on Amazon.com!

Scan me

<u>**Want to read more?**</u>

Follow Author Lacey Love below
to get notifications every time a
new book is released. Want to learn
more about our other erotic series
Girls Who Brunch? Then head to
workingbluepress.com!

Scan me

www.ingramcontent.com/pod-product-compliance
Lightning Source LLC
Chambersburg PA
CBHW031549310726

48971CB00008B/2680